TIMMY TEACUP'S

TERRIFIC AND TERRIBLE TALE

A Story About School and Bullying

Barbara Daniels

Barbara Daniels

Archway Publishing books may be ordered through booksellers or by contacting:

Archway Publishing
1663 Liberty Drive
Bloomington, IN 47403
www.archwaypublishing.com
1 (888) 242-5904

ISBN: 978-1-4808-6481-8 (sc)
ISBN: 978-1-4808-6480-1 (hc)
ISBN: 978-1-4808-6482-5 (e)

Print information available on the last page.

Archway Publishing rev. date: 07/25/2018

Acknowledgements

I would like to thank my wonderful, talented illustrator, Joshua Allen, for making my Timmy Teacup books so special! His pictures are the "heart" of my books helping me win the PINNACLE BOOK ACHIEVEMENT AWARD for Best Children's Picture Book-2018! Thanks, Joshua!

I would also like to thank my 11 year old grandson, Jake, for his enlightened suggestions regarding those illustrations. His input for what to add to the scenes has been inspired & so helpful. Thanks, Jake!

Timmy TeaCup, a plain little white teacup with green spots, lives at 33 TeaCup Lane on the old piecrust table by the fireplace in the dining room. He lives with his Mom, his Grandma, his Great Grandma, and lots of other much more colorful and fancy teacups. One bright and sunny day in August, Timmy heard the human children in the house talking excitedly about starting school the next day. Timmy said to his Mom and Grandma, "Can I go to school, too?" They looked at him and said, "You know what, Timmy – we think you ARE ready to start school." He was SO HAPPY!

His Mom and Grandma decided that the oldest and wisest teacup should do the teaching. That would be Timmy's 94 year old GREAT GRANDMA! She had been a teacher for 50 years before she retired. But, now she was going to come out of retirement to teach Timmy and his friends because she loved Timmy and wanted to help him.

Timmy had four friends who wanted to learn all sorts of new and interesting things at school, too. They were Fred the Fork, Donna the Dish, Sally the Spoon, and Nick the Knife. Timmy's Great Grandma's name was Grannie and she said they would have school on the dining room table next to the old piecrust table by the fireplace in the dining room.

So, Grannie started teaching the very next day – really awesome things about science, geography, history, math, and art. Timmy and his friends were entertained by all of this and couldn't wait for the next day to find out more amazing things.

The months went by smoothly. Everyone was learning a lot and very glad that they had such a wonderful teacher. She was so terrific because she was patient and kind and loving. If someone was having trouble understanding something or needed more time to finish an assignment, she always was very forgiving and helpful.

Unfortunately, one day Grannie got a slight cold and cough and needed to rest for a day or two. She WAS a 94 year old teacup after all! She told everyone to write a story while school was postponed and they would read them out loud when school was in session again.

Timmy was trying to think up an idea for his story when he heard the human kids in the house come home from school. One of the boys named Stevie had been complaining EVERY DAY after school that he didn't like school. But, this day he was really crying and very upset! Here's the story that Timmy wrote after he heard what had happened to Stevie:

[Once upon a time there was a nice little boy named Stevie. He was in third grade. One day he came home from school sobbing. He crouched in the corner and said, "I feel like a big blob of NOTHING!" Obviously, his parents were very sad that Stevie felt that way. They asked him what happened and he said his teacher, Mrs. Goody, was so mean to him and his whole class. He said other kids were crying, too. He told how Mrs. Goody would walk around the room and push kids on the shoulder and say in a very stern voice, "Get to work!" Also, she would yell at the class if they did ANYTHING she didn't like! She expected them to be PERFECT. He said he NEVER wanted to go to school again! He said her name, Mrs. Goody, sounds nice, but she really isn't! Now it made sense why he said he didn't like school! Stevie's parents didn't know what to do. They tried to calm Stevie down and help him feel better. They said he did the right thing telling them what was going on.

The next day, Stevie's parents talked to the principal to see if he could be moved to a different teacher, but the principal said, "No." That's when Stevie's Mom said she would have Stevie stay home and she would "home school" him for the rest of the year. His brothers and sister still went to that same school, but their teachers were nice like Grannie, so they were happy.] That was the end of Timmy's story.

The next day Grannie was feeling much better, so school started up again. Timmy and his friends read their stories and Grannie said they all did an EXCELLENT job. Timmy read his story last and when he was done, Grannie said his story was EXCELLENT, too, and that they should talk a little bit about "bullying".

Timmy had never heard the word "bullying" before. Grannie said it means when someone makes fun of you in a mean way or when someone treats you with disrespect or in a cruel way and then doesn't care if it upsets you. She said usually it's the kids at school or online on the computer or even your brother or sister that are bullies; but, sometimes it can even be TEACHERS that are bullies. Sad, but true! She said Stevie did the right thing by telling his parents, because NO ONE should have to take bullying – EVER. Grannie said, "The lesson for the day to be learned from Timmy's story is to be strong and stand up for yourself. Don't let ANYONE bully you for any reason. You should know the difference between teasing just for fun and mean spirited teasing. And, you should know when someone is really being mean and hurtful. Also, if you see someone else being bullied you should try to help them, too. Be sure to tell your parents, or whoever takes care of you, or someone you trust, all about it, so they can help! Don't try to fix it by yourself!

Then, Timmy said, "I remember, Grannie, when you and Mom and Grandma taught me to "love myself just the way I am." This time, Stevie learned to love HIMSELF enough to ask for help!"

Then the whole class CHEERED!

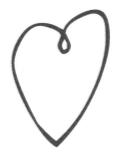

ONE YEAR LATER:

Hi, Kids!

I thought you might want to know how Stevie is doing now. He is still homeschooling with his Mom and loving it. He's learning a lot and is happy! His brothers and sister are still at their regular school and happy where they are, too. So, things have worked out well for Stevie. He is where he needs to be. Maybe someday he will go back to a regular school – maybe not. For now, things are as they should be.

Sometimes Stevie and his Mom do their homeschooling on the dining room table with all of my friends and Grannie and me. That's really fun because we can hear what they are learning that day. One day Stevie learned a special poem that his grandmother wrote. It's called "LOVE YOURSELF". I thought you might like to learn it, too. So, here it is on the next page. I hope you like it!

Your friend,

Timmy Teacup

LOVE YOURSELF

Whether you're thin or fat,
Purple or blue,
Just love yourself,
Because you're **YOU**!